The NOSE BOOK

BY AL PERKINS

ILLUSTRATED BY

Roy McKie

A Beginning Beginner Book

COLLINS AND HARVILL

ISBN 0 00 171208 X
COPYRIGHT © 1970 BY RANDOM HOUSE, INC.,
A BRIGHT AND EARLY BOOK FOR BEGINNING BEGINNERS
PUBLISHED BY ARRANGEMENT WITH RANDOM HOUSE, INC.
NEW YORK, NEW YORK
FIRST PUBLISHED IN GREAT BRITAIN 1971
PRINTED IN GREAT BRITAIN
COLLINS CLEAR-TYPE PRESS: LONDON AND GLASGOW

Everybody
grows
a nose.

I see a nose
on every face.

I see noses
every place!

A nose
between
each pair of eyes.

Noses!
Noses!
Every size.

They grow
on every
kind of head.

They come in blue . . .

. . . and pink

. . . and red.

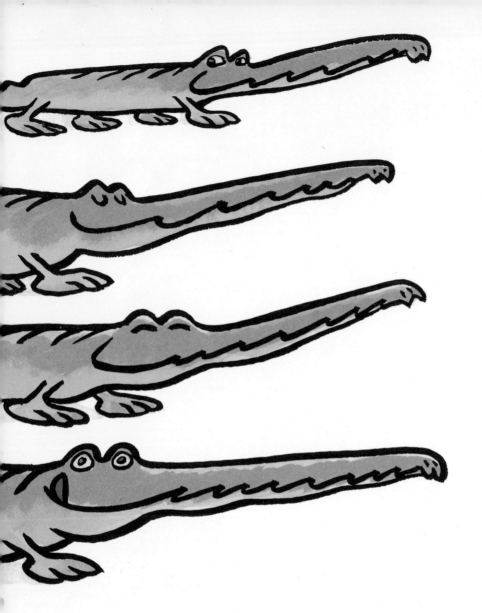

Some are
very, very long.

Some are
very, very strong.

Everywhere a fellow goes,
he sees some
new, new kind of nose.

A nose is useful.
After all . . .

some play horns . . .

. . . and some play ball.

A nose is good
for making holes
. . . in trees

. . . and roofs

. . . and barber poles.

But sometimes
noses aren't much fun.
They sniffle.

They get burned by sun.

A nose gets punched . . .

. . . and bumped on doors

. . . and bumped on walls

. . . and bumped on floors!

Sometimes
your nose
will make you sad.
Sometimes
your nose
will make you mad.

BUT . . .

Just suppose
you had no nose!

Then you
could never
smell
a rose . . .

. . . or pie, or chicken a la king.

You'd never smell a single thing.

And one thing more.
Suppose . . . no nose . . .

Where would
all our glasses sit?
They'd all fall off!
Just THINK of it!

And that's why
everybody grows,
between his eyes,
some kind of nose!